WATERSHIP DOWN

Challenge to Efrafa

Other
Watership Down
fiction adventures

Challenge
to Efrafa

Judy Allen

RED FOX

A Red Fox Book

Published by Random House Children's Books
20 Vauxhall Bridge Road, London SW1V 2SA

A division of The Random House Group Ltd
London Melbourne Sydney Auckland
Johannesburg and agencies throughout the world

Text and illustrations © 1999 Alltime Entertainment Ltd.
and DECODE Entertainment Inc.

www.watershipdown.net

Illustrations by County Studio, Leicester

1 3 5 7 9 10 8 6 4 2

Printed and bound in Denmark by Nørhaven A/S

THE RANDOM HOUSE GROUP Limited Reg. No. 954009

www.randomhouse.co.uk

ISBN 0 09 940385 4

This story represents scenes from
the television series, Watership Down,
which is inspired by Richard Adams'
novel of the same name.

Contents

The Characters of Watership Down

Hazel

The leader of the group, Hazel persuaded his friends to leave their old warren at Sandleford and start a new life elsewhere.

Fiver

One of the youngest rabbits, Hazel's brother Fiver has visions of the future – a gift that sometimes causes him many problems.

Bigwig

A former member of the Sandleford Owsla, Bigwig naturally uses force to settle any disputes and has no time for time-wasters.

Pipkin

The youngest and most vulnerable rabbit, Pipkin is innocent, sweet and adventurous, and a well-loved friend to all the group.

Blackberry

An intelligent doe, Blackberry is a great problem solver and at times of crisis, she is the calm voice of reason.

Hawkbit

Hawkbit is always ready to look on the glum side, but when the going gets tough, his loyalty to the group shines through.

Dandelion

Talker, joker and storyteller, Dandelion is always ready to celebrate the heroic deeds of the warren and El-Arah.

Kehaar

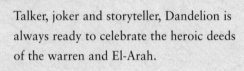

A newcomer to the group, Kehaar thinks he's much cleverer than the rabbits, but infact he can't manage without them.

Hannah

A fearless fieldmouse, Hannah often tends to forget her size and has no problem trading insults with bigger animals.

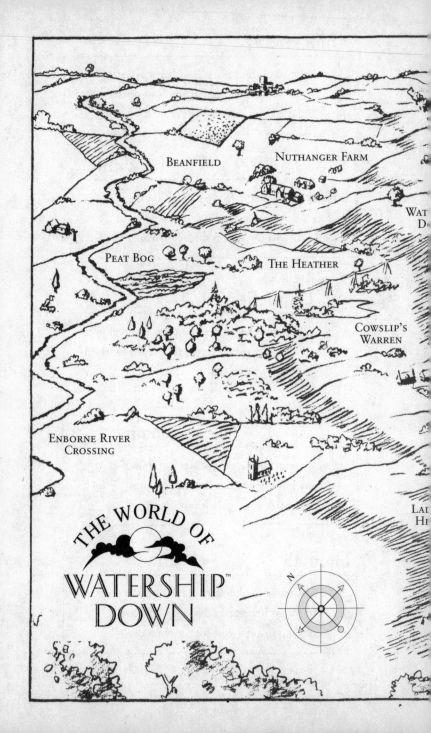

BEANFIELD

NUTHANGER FARM

WAT[...]
D[...]

PEAT BOG

THE HEATHER

COWSLIP'S
WARREN

ENBORNE RIVER
CROSSING

LA[...]
HI[...]

THE WORLD OF
WATERSHIP™
DOWN

N

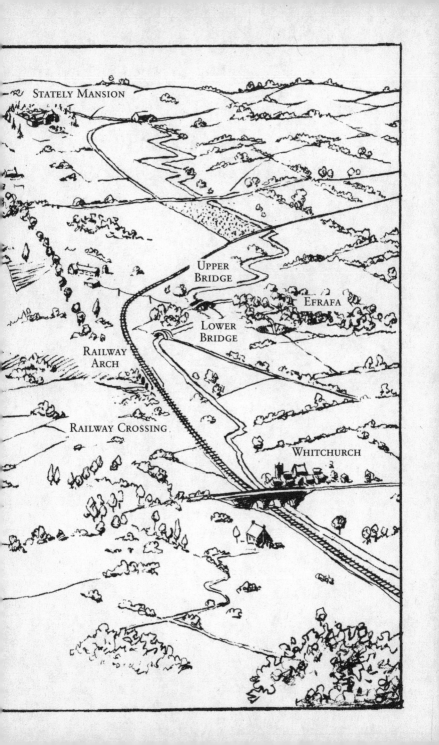

STATELY MANSION

UPPER
BRIDGE

EFRAFA

LOWER
BRIDGE

RAILWAY
ARCH

RAILWAY CROSSING

WHITCHURCH

CHAPTER ONE

Making Plans

Hazel stood outside the warren on Waterhip Down, watching as Bigwig put Fiver, Hawkbit, Dandelion and little Pipkin through their paces.

'Well done, lads,' said Bigwig, when they'd finished. 'You can run as fast, jump as high and hide as well as any rabbit I've ever seen.'

Hazel nodded, pleased. 'Bigwig,'
he said, 'your Owsla is well trained.
We're ready to go back to Efrafa and
rescue Primrose and Blackavar.'

Everyone stared at him in disbelief.
Hawkbit said, 'You're mad!'
and even Bigwig
looked anxious.

Hazel hardly
noticed. He was
thinking about
Primrose.

And in
Efrafa,

Primrose was thinking about Hazel –
and freedom.

She was busy digging an escape
tunnel out of the burrow she shared
with Blackavar. When she stopped to
rest, Blackavar helped her pull a root
across the tunnel entrance, to hide it.

A sudden and terrible roar made them both jump.

'It's General Woundwort,' said Primrose. She crept into the passageway to listen. Blackavar followed nervously.

Woundwort was in the grand audience chamber nearby. They could hear him clearly. 'Campion! Vervain!' he bellowed. 'Send out

more patrols. Find Hazel's warren.
Destroy it. Bring Hazel and Fiver
to me.'

Primrose shivered. Then she
whispered, 'More Owsla on patrol
means that there are less guarding us
here. This is our chance to escape.'

Blackavar's eyes were wide and
fearful. 'But how would we find
Hazel's warren?' he said.

'One thing at a time,' said
Primrose firmly.

'Dismissed!' shouted Woundwort.

Blackavar and Primrose fled,
as Campion and Vervain marched
out of the audience chamber. But
they weren't fast enough and they
were seen.

'That Primrose needs watching,'
said Vervain. 'Her spirit hasn't been
broken yet. We should check her
burrow.'

Campion stayed by the burrow-
opening, but Vervain walked straight
in and right up to Primrose.
'You're a real mess, aren't
you?' he said, looking
at her muddy fur.

'Why should I
groom myself
in this place?'
said Primrose.

'Because it's expected,' said Vervain. 'Wash yourself now!'

Slowly, Primrose began to clean one ear.

'I know you're thinking of escape,' said Vervain. 'Well I hope you try because I look forward to catching you. I'll make you suffer, I promise.'

'Time to move on, Vervain,' said Campion, from the entrance.

Vervain strutted out to join him. 'I'll have that trouble-maker shaking at the sight of me,' he said. 'Just give me time...'

But Campion interrupted. 'That'll do,' he said. 'Treat anyone like that again, and you'll answer to me! Now get moving. We have a patrol to organise.'

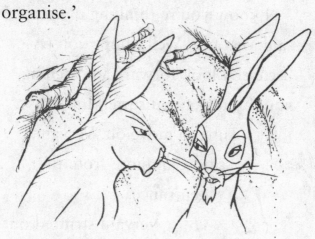

As the two Owsla captains moved away, Woundwort's voice echoed around the warren. 'Efrafa is the only warren. Woundwort is the only leader! Efrafa and Woundwort forever!'

'I've never known him this bad before,' said Primrose.

'He's never met anyone like Hazel before,' said Blackavar.

Primrose smiled. 'Neither have I,' she said. 'We must finish the tunnel and escape.'

'Vervain will kill us,' said Blackavar.

'I won't live here any longer,' said Primrose. 'If I can't have freedom, I'll welcome death.'

Blackavar shuddered. Then he nodded. 'Freedom or death,' he said softly.

CHAPTER TWO

Fox!

Hazel looked at his group of rabbits. 'I need volunteers,' he said.

'You really want to go back to Efrafa?' said Hawkbit.

'I have to,' said Hazel. 'I promised Primrose. Who will come with me?'

Every rabbit raised a paw, and
Kehaar the gull raised one wing.

'Thank you,' said Hazel, touched.
He chose his younger brother,
Fiver, and Bigwig. Then Hawkbit,
Blackberry the doe – and Kehaar
to scout from above.

They travelled fast, talking little, until they reached the woods that led to Woundwort's dark warren at Efrafa.

Then Hazel said, 'Fiver? Any visions yet? I'd like to know if we're going to get through this.'

Fiver shook his head. 'All I see is a grey mist of possibilities,' he said.

'You're a great help!' snapped Hazel. Then he shook himself. 'Sorry, I didn't mean that,' he said.

'I know,' said Fiver. 'You're worried, aren't you?'

'Yes,' said Hazel. 'Everyone's risking their lives for a promise I made.'

'Being a leader means doing what you think is right,' said Fiver. Hazel sighed. 'Trying to do the right thing all the time is difficult,' he said.

23

Kehaar circled low overhead.
'I go ahead and fish in river,' he
squawked. 'You OK without me
watching?'

'We'll be fine,' said Hazel.

'That gull's getting too big for his
beak,' said Bigwig, as they made
their way among the trees.
'Thinks we can't go a
step without him.'

None of them noticed the animal resting in the ferns. None of them heard him padding softly through the woods behind them.

It wasn't until the twisting trail led them to a bubbling stream that Bigwig paused, sniffed the air, and froze. 'Fox!' he whispered.

'This way!' said Hazel, running to a place where the stream tumbled over a rocky shelf, making a small waterfall. 'We can hide behind here. The water will mask our scent.'

As he pushed Fiver, Blackberry and Hawkbit behind the curtain of water, the fox began to race towards them.

'Bigwig,' shouted Hazel. 'Quick!'

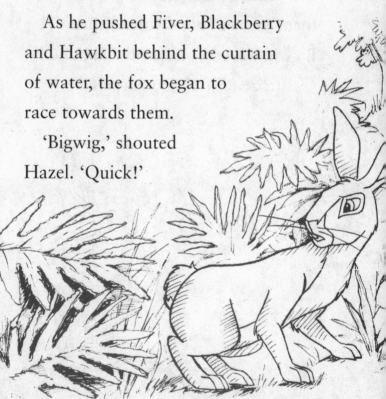

Bigwig hesitated – then swerved away and bolted for the trees, the fox close on his tail.

Moments later, the high-pitched screams of a rabbit tore through the air.

Hazel's eyes widened in horror.

'Bigwig,' he whispered.

'Oh, Bigwig.'

CHAPTER THREE

Blackberry's Discovery

It was some time before Hazel and the others crept out from behind the waterfall. They sat upright, looking, listening and sniffing the air.

A rustling in the undergrowth startled them. Then a familiar figure came pushing through the long grass.

'Bigwig!' said Fiver.

'We thought we'd lost you!'
said Hawkbit.

'We heard screaming!' said
Blackberry.

'The fox was nearly on top of me,'
said Bigwig cheerfully, 'when I
bumped into a couple of
Efrafans. I knocked
them flat and ran,
and the fox got
them both!

Then those two Owsla captains, Campion and Vervain, came along and I had to hide. When Vervain scented fox, he scarpered, but Campion's made of sterner stuff. He stayed and had a look round – but he didn't spot me. As soon as he'd gone I came back here.'

Fiver, Hawkbit and Blackberry were delighted with Bigwig's story, but Hazel looked angry. 'You took an idiotic risk,' he said.

'What's your problem?' said Bigwig, surprised.

'You could have been killed,' said Hazel.

'If I hadn't led him away he'd have found the rest of you,' said Bigwig.

'He might not have,' said Hazel.

Bigwig snorted. 'Your trouble, Hazel,' he said, 'is you want everything safe and nice. Well, the world isn't like that. Come on, let's get to Efrafa.' He bounded off, calling over his shoulder, 'Or are you afraid it's too dangerous?'

The others looked anxiously at Hazel, but he said nothing.

He hopped off after Bigwig, and they followed.

Soon they were at the edge of the
river that bordered Efrafa. Kehaar
was fishing beside a crumbling stone
bridge. They crossed cautiously,
pausing to look down at the river
through a hole in the middle.

There were rabbit tracks
everywhere. Bigwig sniffed them.
'Efrafans,' he said. 'Fresh scent.'

'They'll be back,' said Hazel. 'We
have to think carefully.'

'Think about what?' said Bigwig.
'We've come to get Primrose and
Blackavar.'

'If we go into Efrafa,' said Hazel, 'and a patrol is holding this bridge, we'll be trapped.

Blackberry climbed down the bank and hopped under the bridge. Her voice came up through the hole. 'Hazel, I think I've found our escape route.'

Bigwig stayed where he was, muttering, 'All talk and no action,' but Hazel, Fiver and Hawkbit clambered after her.

Blackberry pointed at something resting on the water, tied to the bank by a strong rope.

'You're right!' said Fiver. 'Hazel – remember when Pipkin and I floated across the river on the log? This is the same kind of thing.'

'Is boat,' said Kehaar, waddling along the bank to look.

'If we float away on this boat-thing, we won't need the bridge,' said Hazel. 'Blackberry, you're brilliant!'

He went back up the bank to tell Bigwig the good news, looked around, then slithered hurriedly down again. 'We'll have to hide here awhile,' he whispered. 'There's an Efrafan patrol heading this way.'

'Where's Bigwig?' said Fiver.

Hazel shook his head. 'He's gone!'

CHAPTER FOUR

A Visitor for Woundwort

Blackavar peered into the dark escape tunnel. 'How are you doing, Primrose?' he called.

A distant muffled voice called back, 'Almost there.' Then a narrow beam of sunlight shone into Blackavar's eyes, and a few moments later Primrose scrambled back down

the tunnel, showering him with
earth.

'You've broken through!' said
Blackavar happily, as they
pulled the root across the
entrance.

'Bad news,' said
Primrose. 'I came up

inside the boundaries of Efrafa, right near a guard-post.'

'We'll have to dig further,' said Blackavar.

'No,' said Primrose. 'The tunnel will be discovered soon. We must take a chance and run for it... as soon as it's dark.'

A sudden roar from Woundwort frightened them both – but he wasn't angry with them. He was in his audience chamber shouting at someone else.

'I'm surrounded by fools,' he bawled. 'Fools! Traitors! Cowards!'

Primrose nudged Blackavar. 'I'm going to listen,' she said.

'Be careful!' said Blackavar.

'We need to know what's happening,' said Primrose, and she crept down the corridor and peeped into the audience chamber.

Vervain was standing in front of Woundwort's throne, quivering.

'You ran at the first sign of danger,' shouted Woundwort.

'I'm sorry, General,' Vervain whimpered. 'There was a fox...'

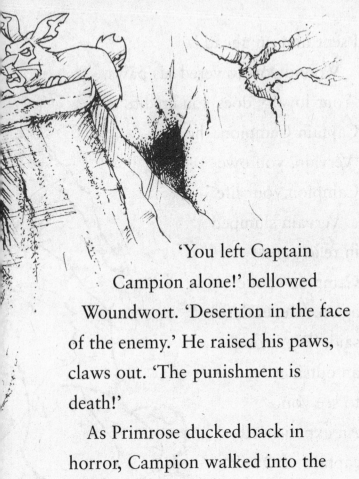

'You left Captain Campion alone!' bellowed Woundwort. 'Desertion in the face of the enemy.' He raised his paws, claws out. 'The punishment is death!'

As Primrose ducked back in horror, Campion walked into the audience chamber from the other side. He bowed respectfully and said, 'General, Vervain didn't desert.

I sent him on ahead.'

Woundwort lowered his paws.
'Your loyalty does you credit,
Captain Campion,' he said.
'Vervain, you owe
Campion your life.'

Vervain slumped
in relief, and
Campion spoke
again. 'General,' he
said, 'I've brought
an outsider
to see you.
An experienced
captain of Owsla.
He wishes to join
our warren.'

'Bring him in,' commanded Woundwort.

Campion beckoned, and a large rabbit with a tuft of fur between his ears stepped forward and stood before the General.

'I have heard,' he said, 'that you are a famous leader of great warriors.'

Woundwort gave him a chilling stare.

'And?' he said.

'And I am a lone warrior, looking for a chief to serve.'

'Your name?' demanded Woundwort.

'Bigwig, sir,' said Bigwig, bowing low. 'Captain Bigwig, at your service.'

CHAPTER FIVE

A Meeting on the Bridge

Woundwort glowered at Bigwig. 'Where are you from?' he demanded.

'Sandleford Warren, sir,' said Bigwig. 'It was destroyed by Man.'

'Man!' Woundwort growled. 'May Frith burn the flesh from his bones.' He looked Bigwig up and down.

'You say you're a warrior?' He
pointed to Vervain. 'Could you
fight him?'

Instantly, Bigwig threw himself at
Vervain, knocked him down and
stood over him. 'Shall I kill him,
General?' he asked politely.

Woundwort smiled unpleasantly.
'Not today,' he said.

Bigwig stepped back and Vervain struggled to his feet, giving him a look of pure hatred.

'All right, Bigwig,' said Woundwort, 'you can stay while I decide if you're good enough. Campion, introduce the new recruit to the ways of Efrafa.'

Primrose, listening outside, flattened herself against the wall as Campion and Bigwig passed. Campion didn't see her, but Bigwig did, and he managed to whisper, 'Hazel says hello!'

Then he
hurried to
catch up with
Campion, while
Primrose skittered
back to Blackavar,
whispering excitedly,
'There's a new rabbit here. He's
come to help us, I know he has.'

As Campion took Bigwig on
a tour of Efrafa, a shadowy figure
followed. Vervain was stalking them
silently, dodging out of sight each
time Bigwig turned round.

'Campion,' said Bigwig at last. 'We're being followed.'

Campion shrugged. 'In Efrafa, someone's always watching,' he said.

'That'll make things difficult,' Bigwig muttered to himself.

Outside, they came upon a group of rabbits feeding. They grazed in orderly rows, watched over by guards.

'Woundwort likes everybody kept in line, doesn't he?' said Bigwig.

'Order and control are necessary,' said Campion. 'Don't you agree?'

'Yes, if you want to stop rabbits thinking for themselves,' said Bigwig, quietly.

Luckily Campion didn't hear. He called to a guard, 'Time's up for the Hind Mark. Get them inside. Bring out the Shoulder Mark.'

Bigwig shook his head sadly as the rabbits filed past, each marked with a scar on the flank.

After a while, he and Campion
came to the old stone bridge.
The guards were nibbling clover
dangerously close to Hazel's hiding
place, but Campion shouted, 'Get to
your posts at once!' and they darted
back up the embankment.

While Campion scolded the
guards, Bigwig moved to the hole
in the bridge. He looked down it,
winked at Hazel, and said, 'I shall
enjoy serving in the Efrafan Owsla,
Campion. Mind if I have a look
around on my own?'

'OK,' said Campion, 'but don't try
to leave.' And the two rabbits moved
off in opposite directions.

Under the bridge, Hazel said,
'Blackberry – stay with the boat. Get
it ready for our escape. Bigwig's
on the inside now – the
rest of us must
help him.'

At that moment they heard
Vervain's voice, right beside the hole.
'Guards!' he said, 'Let's see why
Bigwig was looking down here.'

Within seconds, Kehaar had flown
straight up through the hole,
knocking the Efrafans backwards.
By the time they'd recovered,
Hazel, Hawkbit and Fiver
had scrambled up the
embankment and
disappeared into
the undergrowth.

Bigwig was waiting nearby. 'I'll get Primrose and Blackavar out somehow,' he said.

'We'll meet you in the brambles outside Efrafa,' said Hazel. But before he could say anything about the boat, footsteps sent him diving for cover.

Vervain, flanked by two guards, marched up to Bigwig. 'You're under arrest,' he said triumphantly. 'I'm taking you to General Woundwort.'

CHAPTER SIX

Escape from Efrafa

The guards marched Bigwig into the audience chamber and halted in front of Woundwort on his high throne. Vervain followed with Campion.

'General,' said Vervain eagerly, 'I knew this Bigwig had an odd smell, so I've been following him – and suddenly I was attacked by a ferocious gull.'

Woundwort frowned.

'Sir,' said Vervain, dancing with excitement, 'it was the same gull that helped Hazel and Fiver escape from Efrafa!' He pointed dramatically at Bigwig. 'You and that gull are working for Hazel,' he said. 'You can't deny it!'

'A gull!' said Bigwig scornfully. 'That's quite a story, Vervain! I'd say you're out for revenge! You can't beat me in a fight, so you attack me with lies.'

He leapt at Vervain and would have knocked him down, but Campion pulled him away saying, 'Don't make things worse.'

Woundwort stepped down from his throne and towered over Bigwig. Bigwig stared defiantly back at him.

In a sudden movement, Woundwort slashed out with a forepaw, leaving a bleeding gash on Bigwig's shoulder.

Bigwig didn't flinch, and a
flicker of admiration passed over
Woundwort's face. 'I pronounce you
Captain Bigwig of the Shoulder
Mark,' he said. 'If your loyalty
matches your courage, you'll do
well. As for you, Vervain,
get out of my sight.

Vervain slunk away,
but Campion said,
'Well done, Bigwig,
you're one of us.'

As soon as he could get away on his own, Bigwig found his way to Primrose and Blackavar's burrow, and introduced himself. 'Hazel sent me to get you out,' he said.

'We're ready,' said Primrose. She hopped to the back of the burrow and pulled aside the root. 'We've dug a tunnel.'

'Hazel was right about you,' said Bigwig, impressed.

'But it comes out right by a guard-post,' said Primrose.

'We'll have to risk it,' said Bigwig. 'Hazel and the others are hiding close by. They could be discovered at any time. Let's get going.'

Primrose nodded, but Blackavar shrank back.

'Come on, lad,' said Bigwig, leading the way. 'We'll make it.'

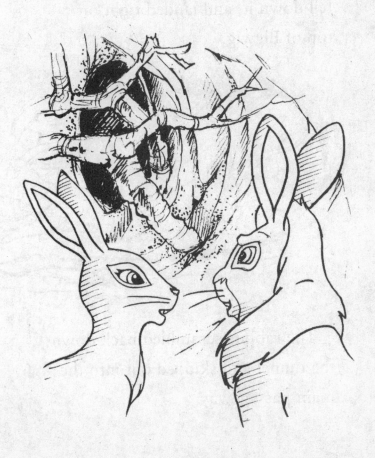

They had almost reached the top
of the tunnel when it happened.
Vervain, inspecting the guard-post
above, trod on the tunnel-opening,
fell down it, and landed right on
top of Bigwig.

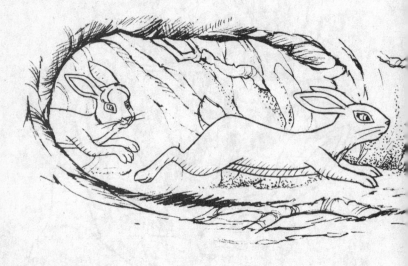

The rabbits scrambled back down
the tunnel and skidded out into the
main passageway.

Vervain's shouts alerted the
Efrafan guards, who ran from every
direction.

'Don't stop for anything!' yelled
Bigwig, racing for the warren
entrance, the other two close behind.

Efrafan guards blocked the
opening, but Bigwig knocked them
aside, and the next second the three
rabbits were out in the sunshine,
running hard.

Hazel, Fiver and Hawkbit broke
clear of the brambles and joined the
mad dash, as Kehaar rose, shrieking,
into the sky above.

The Efrafan Owsla burst out of
the warren in hot pursuit, led by

Vervain and Campion. Woundwort
himself kept pace, his face twisted
with rage. 'Kill them!' he roared.
'Kill them all!'

As the rabbits dashed for the river, the bridge-guards prepared to stop them, but at the last minute Hazel led them in a slithering rush down the embankment.

'They're trapped,' roared Woundwort, as his Owsla skidded to a halt around him.

Fiver, Hawkbit, Blackavar and
Primrose dived into the boat, while
Blackberry chewed frantically at
the mooring rope, and Hazel and
Bigwig turned to face Campion
and Vervain.

'I'm sorry it had to end this way,'
said Campion.

But Vervain snarled, 'I've got you
at last!'

The mooring rope snapped.

'Now!' shouted Fiver.

Hazel and Bigwig ran along the bank and leapt into the boat, just as the current caught it and swept it away.

On the bridge, Woundwort reared up on his haunches, bellowing his rage and frustration to the sky. Beside him, Vervain spluttered with fury – but Campion watched the escape with a small smile on his face.

The boat drifted away from Efrafa, between reed-beds and willow trees, with Kehaar gliding peacefully above.

Hazel looked fondly at Primrose.

'You're free,' he said softly.

'Free,' nodded Primrose.

'Just as you promised.'

And the setting sun turned the river water to gold.

Glossary
OF ESSENTIAL RABBIT WORDS

Buck   A male rabbit

Doe   A female rabbit

Efrafa   The name of General
              Woundwort's warren

El-Arah   The shortened name of the
              rabbit hero, El-ahrairah. The
              many stories of El-Arah are
              an inspiration to all rabbits

Elil   Enemies of rabbits; like foxes,
              hawks and weasels

Flayrah   Good food; like carrots,
              cabbages and lettuces

Frith   The sun; a god to the rabbits

Frithmas   The rabbits' Christmas
                    celebration; it is celebrated
                    with a great feast

Inle   The moon; when it is time
                    for a rabbit to die, the Black
                    Rabbit of Inle comes to
                    fetch him

Owsla   A group of strong brave
                    rabbits who are trained to
                    defend the warren

Silflay   Eating outside the warren;
                    usually at dawn or dusk

Warren   The network of burrows
                    where rabbits live

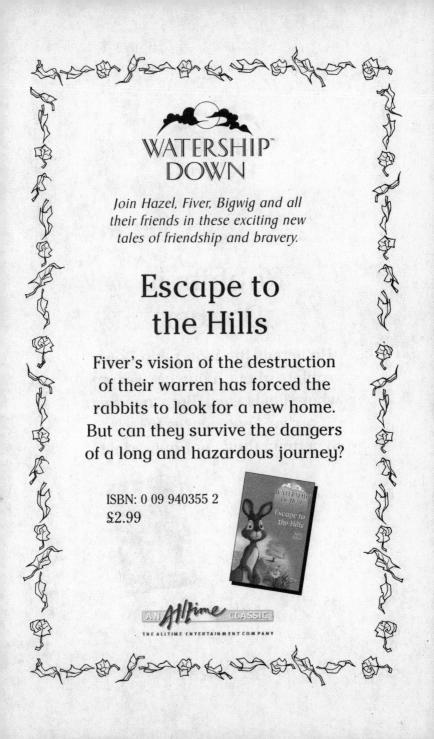

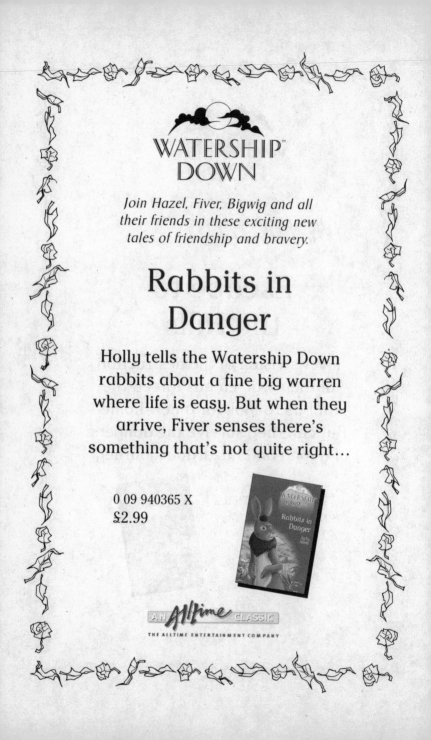

WATERSHIP DOWN

Join Hazel, Fiver, Bigwig and all their friends in these exciting new tales of friendship and bravery.

Rabbits in Danger

Holly tells the Watership Down rabbits about a fine big warren where life is easy. But when they arrive, Fiver senses there's something that's not quite right...

0 09 940365 X
£2.99

WATERSHIP™ DOWN

*Join Hazel, Fiver, Bigwig and all
their friends in these exciting new
tales of friendship and bravery.*

COMING SOON

The Hidden World

When Hazel, Hawkbit and
Fiver fall down a hole in their
warren, they find themselves
buried in an underground
tunnel. But where does it lead
and can they find a way out?

AVAILABLE MARCH 2000

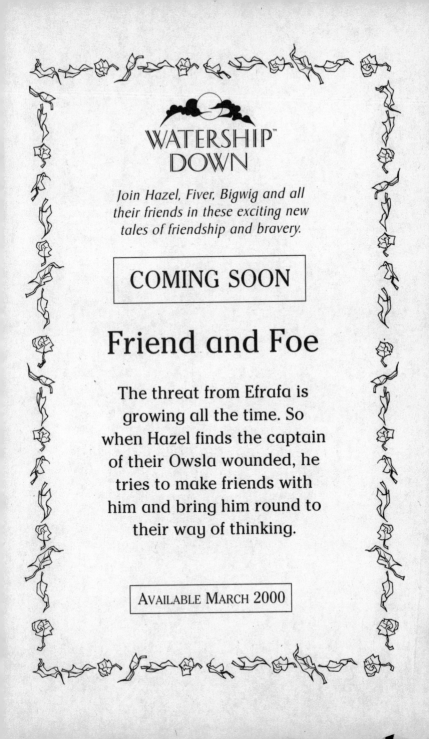

WATERSHIP DOWN

Join Hazel, Fiver, Bigwig and all their friends in these exciting new tales of friendship and bravery.

COMING SOON

Friend and Foe

The threat from Efrafa is growing all the time. So when Hazel finds the captain of their Owsla wounded, he tries to make friends with him and bring him round to their way of thinking.

AVAILABLE MARCH 2000